GRANDMOTHER THORN

by Katey Howes   art by Rebecca Hahn

Ripple Grove
Press

GRANDMOTHER THORN
lived in the very first house
on the very straight road
to Shizuka Village.

With painstaking precision and infinite care,
she maintained her plants and path.
Every leaf, every pebble had its place.

So greatly did Grandmother Thorn value perfect order
that she forbade the birds to nest in her trees.

Quiet prevailed in Shizuka Village. Unless, that is, someone disrupted Grandmother Thorn's carefully raked gravel or snapped a stem from one of her cleverly clipped trees.

Then the old woman shouted in a voice as gravelly as her path.
She shook her rake and muttered for the rest of the day.

The only one immune to Grandmother Thorn's anger was Ojiisan, who brought his friend sweets from the village.

One of Ojiisan's shoulders tipped lower than the other. His left foot twisted sharply inward. When he walked the path to Grandmother Thorn's door, his weak foot dragged a trail in the gravel.

Grandmother Thorn never shouted at her friend, no matter how he disturbed her straight lines and smooth curves.

After hot tea and quiet conversation,

Grandmother Thorn followed Ojiisan back to the road, smoothing the path behind him.

One steaming summer afternoon, Ojiisan sat, resting his sore joints. A traveling merchant came to the village, bringing with him fruits that no one had ever seen.

The moment Ojiisan tasted the deep-red berries with many seeds, he thought of his friend Grandmother Thorn and her love of sweets.

"Kind traveler, I will give you an extra coin to deliver this last basket of berries to my friend. But I must warn you—only stand at the gate and call for her. If you disrupt her garden, you will regret it!"

The merchant did not listen well.

He stepped past Grandmother Thorn's fence and marveled at the beauty and the symmetry he saw.

He reached out to pick a cluster of creamy-white blossoms.

The sound traveled straight to Grandmother Thorn's ears, unleashing her anger.

She sprang up and grabbed her rake, dashing toward the traveler and shouting wildly.

The merchant sprinted away, dropping the basket of berries.

Grandmother Thorn continued to yell as she gathered up the tumbling fruit.
She did not notice one berry that rolled into a dimple in the ground.

Many days passed before Ojiisan felt limber enough to visit again, carrying a parcel of sweet dorayaki. It surprised him to see his friend kneeling by her fence, rags wrapped around her hands.

"What are you doing to that seedling?" he asked.

"Pulling it out!" Grandmother Thorn snapped. "It did not have my permission to grow!"

A week later, Ojiisan spotted his friend crouched in the same place.
"I must not have removed the entire root," she said, digging up the offending vine.
"I will certainly get it this time."

Each time Ojiisan visited, he found Grandmother Thorn more consumed by her battle
with the stubborn sprout. He began to worry.

"My friend, have you considered that everything on earth sooner or later meets its match?"

"Excellent point, Ojiisan," Grandmother Thorn answered.
"Perhaps you might explain it to the plant."

Grandmother Thorn's voice no longer grated as coarse and hard as gravel.
It drooped like an old tree, withering in drought.
Her hair tangled like the thorny vines invading her fence.

Her garden fell into disrepair. One morning, she did not rake the path.

The villagers carried her to the home of her eldest niece where she slept for many months.
While she rested, Ojiisan cared for her garden as well as he could.

Spring came again before Grandmother Thorn grew strong enough to return home.

Ojiisan came to her one afternoon with a gift: a basket of the sweet, deep-red berries.

"Where did you find these?" Gramdother Thorn asked. "I dreamed of them all winter long."

"Come with me," Ojiisan answered.
"I have something to show you."

Grandmother Thorn stared in silence.

At last, a smile conquered her frown.

"It was truly said, my friend, that sooner or later everything on earth meets its match."

For Michael, who knew I could. —K.H.

For my loves: brian kelly hahn, Otto Kitty,
and Quimby Sweetheart. —R.H.

First Edition 2017
Library of Congress Control Number 2017933822
ISBN 978-0-9913866-9-7

10 9 8 7 6 5 4 3 2 1
Printed in South Korea

This book was typeset in Cochin
The art was painted, sewn,
and crafted by hand
Book design by Rebecca Hahn

Ripple Grove
Press
Portland, OR
RippleGrovePress.com